To Li[l]

Friends

Graneg Louis Jackson

MID NIGHT SURFER

SURFER

Cramer Louis Jackson

Ordering Information:

For orders and inquiries, please contact:
1-888-375-9818
www.toplinkpublishing.com
bookorder@toplinkpublishing.com

Printed in the United States of America

Longtime, Oceanside resident, surfer, lifeguard, and fireman Cramer Jackson has been a Monday volunteer docent for some time. A CSM member since the museum first came to Oceanside, Cramer now enjoys taking visitors on a tour through the exhibits and teaching them some of the finer points of surfing. "I love being a docent because, first of all, I like people. The guests seem to like the stories I tell and they frequently ask good questions."

His passion for surfing is undeniable. He knew he wanted to be a surfer from the time he saw the Hawaiian beachboys catching waves in the 1950's newsreels at the local movie house. When he was about 11 or 12 he hung out at the Pier and there he met the charismatic lifeguard who was to be his role model and mentor Doug Tico. Doug was in charge of the rescue boards.

"When we kids wanted to go surfing we had to borrow big old boards from the lifeguards, but you know that probably made me a better surfer. In those days you didn't learn in the soup, you had to go out to the green water to prove you were a macho kid. It was dangerous just paddling out when the guys wiped out and those heavy boards were loose. You had to pay attention."

Asked what he remembered about his friend, Phil Edwards, Cramer said, "He was a star to begin with. He could do anything on a board. How we envied his skill!" About LJ Richards: "LJ is a fabulous surfer and very talented physically. He could stand on a surf mat and surf it beautifully."

In the summer 56 was THE SUMMER OF YOUNG LOVE I was 17 life Guarding when I met Gloria Neil who was 15 1/2 and we had a wonderful time on the beach in the water and in the moon light. She was the most beautiful girl I ever have seen. I will never forget Gloria.

This book is dedicated to Gloria Neil Roberts

(we were not the ones in the book)

ACKNOWLEDGEMENTS

Some special thanks for the skills and
creative help in putting together this book
And to all that gave me encouragement
To the Oceanside Yacht Club members
To the North Cost Vettes (corvette)
In a big way The California Surf Museum
Most of all those that I Surfed with

In one of days in the 50ths, there is a nice on shore breeze that help cool down the hot sand that beach goers so that some that it would be bearable to walk to the ocean and that would mean there would be many people a lot of work for the lifeguards. One named Jim and the other guard was called by his surfing name Surfersam who was the first to arrive at the tower and begin placing the equipment need for the day needs. He was putting out the lifeguard buoys and swim fends when Jim arrives and says to Surfersam "Hey I sorry am late. I was playing around with my girlfriend to long." Surfersam answers Jim, " I don't blame you. She is so beautiful, but you can make it up at my lunch time. I have a woman coming to see me about taking surfing lessons. It's always a good way to make some more money. I hope she's not overweight and can't swim. A lot of women I get to teach, think that surfing is easy and a good way to lose fat and have fun and because surfing looks easy and and but find it takes a lot work and they give it up. Some have to stop because parents think we surfers are the scum on Earth, and there is some guy that think girls shouldn't be in the surf because they would be getting in their way and that surfing are only for men. I think that as years go by some girls show up the guys." Jim says, "I think most people don't even know what surfing is. All they think that all we are is surf bums and to be dome not to amount to anything. I think some day they will wake up and see that we have it right and we might even start a up a surfing club." Surfersam said, "Did you know we missed a day of history in that there were fourteen guys surfing at the same time and we missed it. That had to be all the guys on the coast at one time and we miss it.

As the tie went on and a couple rescues Surfersam told Jim that he would have to go in the restaurant to meet the lady that wants to learn to surf so the tower is his.

Surfersam walks into the restaurant and sits down and orders some food and look around to see if the girl he is to meet is there now that the time they were to meet and sees a very large girl with a ton of food around her table mostly sweets. She sees him and smiles at him. Surfersam thinks to himself, "This is going hard job if it that's her. Just as Surfersam looks around to get out of the restaurant before he has to deal with the large lady. Surfersam sees a very, very beautiful woman who enters the restaurant and she sees Surfersam and walks up to and says, "Hi Surfersam." He is so stunned he has known beautiful women but none as beautiful as her. She tells him, "I am here. I am here for you to teach me to become the best woman surfer every and I have given myself my surfer name is Saltwatersally." Surfersam looked at her, says I would love to make you the best woman surfer in the world and I will have one thing right now Saltwatersally. "So you know how to swim?" Saltwatersally responds, "Yes I have ten trophies in swimming contest but now I want to take it to the next step and I was reading a book with a story about your life guarding and all the people you have saved and all about your surfing and here I am ready to start today. I will be back so we could start with a lesson." He says, "Ok" and smiles. Surfersam smiles and says, "see you soon." Saltwatersally smiles at him and says, "Soon is a good word." And smiles again and departs.

Surfersam tell Jim about Saltwatersally and says, "Be careful you do not fall off the tower." There were not much going on the beach other than some light first aid of a stubbed toe but changed when Saltwatersally walked up to the tower in a couple surf boards and in string bikini looking like some Goddess and the ladies wished they could be as beautiful as she is. Jim looked at but did not fall of the tower. An hour later, a small boat over turned and with too many people were on board and Jim and Surfersam went into action on paddle boards to them. The people on the beach were watching the action while all the people and loved ones of those that in were in the boat standing watching closer when the lifeguards saved those that were on the boat. People were cheering and when Surfersam caring a small child, put the child down, the child came running to his mother, when Saltwatersally came up to Surfesam, the mother of the child told Saltwatersally, "For Peat sakes kiss your boyfriend for me." Saltwatersally ran to him, put her arms around him, kiss him for her and she did in the most passion that all the people were looking with amazement of what passionate love she had for him, and there more cheers and hand clapping and weaseling. All the people with cameras were coming over taking pictures of the lifeguards and all wanted pictures of Saltwatersally kissing Surfersam.

After all was over and the pictures were taking were over, Saltwatersally and Surfersam went down the beach where she could take her first surfing lesson. When Saltwatersally gab her surfboard and ran into the surf with her Board broadside to the wave and of course the board bumped her head. Saltwatersally was fine just a little red spot where the board hit her head. Surfersam said to her, "Well now you learned your first lesson never turn your board broad broadside." Surfersam took Saltwatersally where she could lay down on the board in the water and Surfersam held the board where she could have good balance and tells her "Just jump up as soon as you can when I will push you into the wave." She did as he told her and she yield with joy. She was stoked to learn more. Surfersam was concerned for her safety, he though he should show her how to get though the waves he explained to her how to jump waves and how to dive under the waves. Saltwatersally decides she wants to try diving under the waves so Surfersam shows how by making the dive just before the wave gets to him and he pop up on the other side of the wave. Saltwatersally's timing is off and she dives into the mass of white water and she finds out it is like being in washing machine where she is bounce up and down and all-around and she pops up and takes a deep breath not knowing the she had lost her top freeing her beautiful breast and how much more it makes her look like a goddess and she laughs and says, "Well less drag now" and she shemmy's for him. Knowing that he will have to walk with her back on the beach to were her things are, he dives under the water to look for her bathing suit top is but can't find it. Surfersam thinks to himself, "If I am lucky maybe it will wash up on the beach." As he comes out of his diving, he looks for her and does not see her anywhere and he sees her pop out of the ocean and says to him. "Oh there you are. You were under the water so long I thought something happen, may be a shark got you." (she did not know that he is a champ at free diving) While she was talking to him, she did

7

not see that wave was about to hit her. He "yield" but it was too late the wave slammed her and she went over and over. When she got her feet on the ground, she took a deep breath and shuck herself to get some sea weed off er and noticed that she now lost the bottom of her bathing suit. Surfersam when he saw her , Surfersam had to say, "It looks like the wave broke your string." She said to him, "I always wanted to go skinny dipping so now I think it's time to jump waves together." Surfersam said, YES! (He wanted to say, "Yes, yes. Yes!")

Learning to jump waves is very important in walking out in the small surf and can be very romantic. Sometimes a bigger wave shows up so Surfersam has to go under water to help Saltwatersally jump up high enough. When a very strong wave is coming at them, Saltwatersally grabs Surfersam and holds him very tight her. More may have happened but Surfersam still had his lifeguard suit on and if it did come in off and could not find it, it would be bad for him if people on the beach would see two naked people walking to the lifeguard tower. Of course, if is a clothing optional beach it be ok. Surfersam remembers when he had problems somewhat like this, were neither notice that the girl he was teaching lost her top and nobody notice walking back to the tower. Surfersam made a seaweed skirt for Saltwatersally for her then he had her to carry her surfboard under her arm and turn the board trod your breast. This worked well and they got to the tower were Surfersam gave her one his T shirt and a towel to put around waste. Jim and Surfersam put things away and closed the tower. Jim went to his car and Saltwatersally went with Surfersam yo his car and drove away to Saltwatersally's house. Saltwatersally says to him, "come on in and see my house." He answered, "Shure." So they enter the house. In the house, it was very clean with wonderful bamboo chairs and coaches with a lot of her panting on the wall and he saw a picture of him on the wall of him coming out of the water with his board under his arm. He thinks it is interesting that it shows that she was at least interested in him before she met him.

Saltwatersally looks at his feet and at her feet and says to him, "We got a lot of sand on our feet that we need to wash off and we need a shower to clean the salt off our body's." Surfersam answers her, "Ok you go ahead and then I will be next." Saltwatersally says, "The water bill here is so high I have to save on any way I can so I want you to join me in the shower, besides, you ave seen me without anything on so you should not be shy, so man up and join me in the shower." He responds to her and says, "OK let's do it and have some fun and get really clean (with a smile)." She looks at him with a smile that would light any city and with a giggle their clothes come off and into the shower they go. The shower lasts such a long time that she did not save any money on the water bill. After the shower they come out to dry each other off they know that they are so much in love that would last forever. The clothes do not go on and both go into the kitchen to have something to eat that takes a long time because each time they look at each other, they have to kiss with passion. They end up after eating in her bedroom together turn into a nap.

After the nap, Surfersam has to go home to take care of the normal things like paying bills before they are overdue. They hug and kiss and say goodbye to each other knowing that their lives will never be the same but are in a new chapter called love.

As Surfersam drives home, he turn on his radio and hears love song like he had never heard them before and he sang them as they came on the radio. He knew that he has really going to teach her to be a good or better surfer so they could surf together.

Saltwatersally had on her CD player, of love songs, as she cleans her home and at times would dance with her broom and wonder if he liked to dance. She made up her mind that she was going to learn to be a really good surfer so she be surfing with him.

The next day, Surfersam walking to the tower, he could not stop thinking about

Saltwatersally and when he got to the tower, Jim was there and said, "Hay I am here on time this time." Then he looked at Surfersam and said you look different. And stopped and then said, "I know what it is, YOU'RE IN LOVE. And he laughed." Surfersam said back to him, "Oh can't a guy be in love without everyone knowing about it?" Jim laughed again and said, "NO" and laughed. Surfersam said to Jim, "GET TO WORK!" Jim went to work but was still laughing inside.

As the day went along, it's about noon when Saltwatersally showed up at the beach with her surfboard and new bikini on and a gowning smile on her face and everyone could tell that she was deeply in love with Surfersam. She was bringing food for the two lovers and Jim. Jim was felt horned that she thought about Surfersam's Life Guard partner. While they were eating, she said to Jim, "I told some of my girlfriends about how handsome you are and a hero like Surfersam and if you like, I can bring some beautiful girls for them to meet you." Jim responds to her and says, "That is very nice of you to think of doing that but I don't think my Freon say would want that. We planned to get married next month, but it was sweet of you to offer to do that." Surfersam says, "It's kind of wonderful that you want to be helpful to the people that are very important in our life and we will be friends for life." Saltwatersally says, "Thank you and you soon to be wife."

At that very minute, a young boy falls off surf mat and is in a strong rip tide seeming for help and splashing all around trying to staying above the water. People from all over the beach stand up to see what is going on. Some of them run closer to get a better look as Surfersam jumps off the life guard tower and grabs his fins and rescue can and with his fins behind puts them on and the shoulder strap on and the rescue tower behind swim very fast in the rip tide current, he arrived just in time and grab the boy's wrist and pulls him up out of the water, hold on to him till they got to shore and put the down as his mother with tears in her eyes grabs son and yells to

Saltwatersally, "For Pete sacks give your hero boyfriend a kiss for me." Saltwatersally ran to Surfersam and put her arms around him and with loving passion gave him a kiss that would last forever in their memories and all the people that were watching the rescue and her love for Surfersam with the kiss clap their hands and with cheers and whistle for the lovers. Every person that had a camera took pictures of Saltwatersally kissing Surfersam. In the morning, newspaper on the front page with the story of the rescue and a big picture of the kiss from Saltwatersally to life guard Surfersam. From that time, people watched them being such lovers ever where they went.

Jim and his girlfriend were to get married that next month but there are problems in the families on how the wedding should go on and who should not be invited and who would be invited and which church it should be in. They decided to elope so to have a loving wedding but before they were to go, they went to Saltwatersally's house for a small party of best friends. The party ending in hugs and kisses and blessing for their new life together. Surfersam would miss Jim the most not being in the Life Guard tower with him, he would and would be looking forward to Jim to be in the tower as a married man. Surfersam hopes the life guard the city is sending to take Jim's place will be as good as Jim. There were so many young men trying to be in the guard with guard Surfersam that the man was there so early he had every thing done to start ready to get started and of course he told his girl friends that he was going to guard with Surfersam. The new guard's girlfriends show up, the girls clapped their hands and cheered and took pictures of her and got her to sign her autograph. When Saltwatersally gave Surfersam a hug and a short kiss, the girls were there with their cameras again to get the picture of her kiss. The young life guard had to tell the girls that is very nice of you to think of doing that but, they should remember they have keep their eyes on the swimmers so enjoy the beach, work on your tan and have fun with your friends, we want you here but we have to watch the water.

Saltwatersally knows Surfersam will miss Jim so she decides she will work hard to learn surfing so his mind will be on her to progress and this would bring them even closer together and a new way of having fun together.

Surfersam is surprised how fast she is leaning to do cut backs no storks take offs beautiful nose rides and 360s pull outs. Surfersam thinks to himself, "This woman is one smart woman. Now I know why she picked the name Saltwatersally she, new more that I thought she did." Surfersam says to himself, "BOY DO I LOVE THIS WOMAN AND ARE WE GOING TO HAVE FUN TOGETHER. THANK YOU, GOD, FOR SENDING HER TO ME.

That night after their shower together and they get out of naked and dripping wet, Surfersam grabs a little box he did from her and get on one knee and opens the little box that has a ring in it and he look up at her and the tears start pouring out her eyes because she knows what he's going to say. He says,

"Saltwatersally, will you marry me?" she breaks into a full crying and says YES, YES, YES, I LOVE YOU SO MUCH !!!" she gets down on one knee, grabs him and kisses him then they both stand up holding each other and continues kissing.

Now that they decided to live together at her house they could save money for their planning their marriage knowing would take time to save the amount they needed to take some of the stress off and have fun they went to the dog pound they found the cutest dog and decided it would be great to have to have fun with to get a way not to get to stressed about money and work and planning. The dog was such a delight for them to share and receive more love in the house. It was time to name the dog so Saltwatersally and Surfersam looked at each other and smiled and both said at the same time, "Wipeout!" When Surfersam was life guarding Saltwatersally would take Wipeout out into the water and put him on the surfboard and got him to learn how to dog surf. All the kids at the beach loved Wipeout and took turn putting him on the surf board so he could ride the wave. The dog was so good at dog surfing that Saltwatersally and Surfersam would have no trouble finding someone to take care of him if they had to work on surfing which was good and knew they could have fun with Wipeout when they got home.

Now that they know that are going to get married and needed to keep it quiet and work on getting great surfing and able do any new surfing moves and even coming up with their new surfing moves. They even study movies what moves of others could do moves so that could do them too. They soon were becoming famous and their love for each other and they were watched for the romance of surfing of their love. They got so good at surfing that people would go to the beach just to see the two lovers surf. And Wipeout had a small show as well.

The time came for the wedding and it was starting at the beach with their friends and anybody at the beach that wanted to see it could. Surfersam looked so handsome in his suit and Saltwatersally she was so beautiful in a stunning wedding dress walking down the beach to the water line there they were said their wedding vales then after the kiss, they had a quick take off of their clothes and were in their swim suits and two people placed surfboard for them, the two now married couple picked up the surfboards and they took them out into the ocean and paddle out the waves. Then their surfing friends paddle out with flowers on their boards. Their timing was great when Surfersam and Saltwatersally were surfing together on the same wave, the other surfers threw their flowers onto the wave. At the same time, a group of singers and dancers from Hawaii sang on loud speakers their love songs and the Holla dancer dance soon trucks came and tables and chairs were sat up and food trucks arrived with the food for the people. A bell rang for the people to come out of the water and all the surfers came out of the water and waited till Surfersam and Saltwatersally got out of the water and all got in line and walked to the food line but stopped for the couple to be seated and then everyone was seated and a minister from Hawaii gave blessing to the love of all the people here and to then to the young couple and for their love for each other and for all that were here for their wedding. As the dinner was ending another table was set up and another truck showed up and carefully places a long cake as long as a surf board and behind the cake was place of a statue of the two.

Surfersam and Saltwatersally step up to table and cut the cake and crossed arms and gave the other a bit of the cake. After they finish the cake, a limo drove up and Surfersam thanked those that worked so hard to put this all together then he ask for GOD's blessing on them. Then Saltwatersally said, "Thank you all for making a young girl's dream to be more than what I could dream and be more than I ever hoped for. I love you all and may God bless you." The couple waved at the people as they got into the limo and the people were waving and cheering and throwing flowers and the kids were cheering because they were lining up for cake. People were taking pictures of all the wedding and now as they got into the limo and it started off the loud speakers played love songs as people put things back, others making their way back to where they came from. Some went back into the ocean to surf and some took Wipeout to surf and people took more pictures this time of Wipeout.

The limo enters the highway that goes along the coast and after a half hour and slows down and turns on the car's blinker in order to drive on to a road passing a sign that says PRIVATE ROAD, the limo travels the road till it gets to wall made of marble with bright red brick on top continues till it comes to large gate that opens as the limo nears it. The limo continues this driving in the direction of a very large Spanish style house, three stories high with a look out room with cameras in order to know who is approaching the home and enters the hoarse shoe drive way stopping at the front doors of the building with people standing there ready to open the limo's door and to take the suit cases and lode them on the cart and takes them to the room where the couple will be staying. At the front door is the owner of the house waiting for the couple to make their way to him.

As the couple make their way to the owne r, the couple notice a beautiful water fountain with statues of Saltwatersally with her being held over head of Surfersam on a surfing board with water spraying in a way that looks like an ocean wave.

"Hallo, hallo, hallo! Welcome to my house. I was talking on the phone with Surfersam and he was telling me that he was marrying the most beautiful woman in the world so, don't tell my wife that I told you that Surfersam was right. You are the most beautiful woman in the world." He said to them. Saltwatersally blushes and then smiles at him then hugs him and she says very quietly, "I will keep you safe and will not tell your wife what you said to me, I would tell her that she is such a lucky woman to have such a man as you are."

They laugh. He said to them, "After Surfersam told me about you two getting married, my wife thought it would be romantic for us to have you own the house while we take little honeymoon back where we met each other. We also thought you two would like to surf our nice waves in front of our house without anyone to be in your way, so we bought a couple surfboards and we thought it be a way to thank Surfersam for saving our lives and of all our family when our boat was hit by a rogue wave that we all were going to go under, GOD bless Surfersam and you too as his new wife." Saltwatersally cried and went right to Surfersam and kissed him and thanked him for saving these wonderful people.

They all went into the house and Saltwatersally got to meet the owner wife and they hit it off right away as if she was part of the family. After that Saltwatersally and Surfersam were introduced to all the people that work there and a list of their names and what kind of work they would be doing. Then they were showed their room, a large room overlooking the coast line.

There were a lot of excitement in the house with newlywed first honeymoon and the older wed honeymoon at the dinner table talking about surfing and about going to where they first met and traveling back the beautiful places and the new place so after dinner it was time for early bedtime from wedding and travel for Saltwatersally and Surfersam. The owners of the house were ready for bed as well after getting for Surfersam and his new wife and getting ready for their trip back to romance.

In the morning had put love harts on the wall and love songs playing in the background and at the end of breakfast there were a lot thank yous, hugs, and kisses, and waves as the owners drove away.

The first thing the newlyweds did was to check out the surf and they were very happy how the waves were braking that they went back, got on their swim suits and the women that worked at the house were trying to take a look at Surfersam, his in shape life guard body and the men were eyeing Saltwatersally in bikini like they all agreed they were the best couple they ever seen and when the two were surfing, it was like none they ever had seen. The surfing was so good that the workers would work as fast as they could just all take an hour just to see them surf.

As the weeks went by so fast, the owner were home after they have the romance increased and had lot of stories to tell everyone. The workers were very happy the owners had a great fun and enjoyed their trip. The Owners ask if Surfersam and Saltwatersally enjoy their time in the house. The workers were excited to that couple enjoyed every thing and mostly surfing the waves. They told them they want them to stay a little longer to see them surf and invite your friends to come and see them surf as well.

The home owner and friends enjoy the surfing of Saltwatersally's skills and can surf so well with Surfersam that they decide to set up a beach show and so people start to notice the sport of surfing and how much Surfersam and Saltwatersally love each other. After every show, more and more people show up to see them surf. Soon they and would charge to be able to find a place where you be able to tricks and surfing moves up and down the board they would be on the same wave and be close enough to jump and trade surfboards at the same time. And being able to do no stork take off together on a large wave together. They became more, more famous for their surfing and their romantic ways. The world became very interested in them too, by people taking movies about of them so Surfersam no longer need to be a life guard because money was pouring in from the surfing shows and they were payed for interviews on TV. In about the same time, a new movie came out named Gulitt and the whole world wanted to be surfers. Surfing now became a billion dollar industries around the world.

In many countries, they were making their beached look like California beaches and in deserts guys could not get dated if they did not have surfboards on their cars and they knew surfers were with the girls and notice that if they wanted to meet a girl, they had to become surfers. The guys that were making surfboards in their garage making as high as $10,000 a day and they had orders to fill and were as behind by three to four months.

Trouble started with all these new surfers in the water and some though that they were so great to themselves that they did not think that surfing had rules and could do anything they wanted to and did not obey what was the main one that was, "If someone is in the peak of the wave that is his wave and you not snake (steal) his wave they went ahead and snaked it this became problems because the older surfers obeyed the rule and it caused fights in the water and on the shore. Many of the new surfers were rude and would go when at a surfing contest interfered and of surfing skill surfing show was going on, causing more fights and injuries. The time came when a rude surfer got Saltwatersally's way that angered Surfersam and had to attack the rude surfer to save Saltwatersally from harm.

Surfersam and Saltwatersally thought that to many surfers were in the day time that they would have surf at night using lights on their surfboards and at times in different colors and spot lights so the people on the shore see them, and in this way could have a way to add music to the show. The show was a big hit, people from everywhere came to see the show and all that saw it, and fell in love with Saltwatersally and Surfersam.

One night some drunks thought that it would be funny if they turn off the lights and music off by setting the generator on fire.

This caused panic among the people that came to see the show. The police were called and arrested the drunks that cause the lights and music go out. Someone yield to the police to shine their spot light to the shore line and there were two surfboards washing up the sand.

Someone screams. "OH NO IT'S Surfersam's and Saltwatersally's!!!" At the sound of that voice, Surfersam looked to his side and there Saltwatersally next to him on a white surfboard heading to a far away light and and Saltwatersally looks at Surfersam and she smiles at him and says, "I do believe we are heading to heaven." And Surfersam smiles and says, "I do believe you are right." And then there is the sound of angels singing and they are in a place of white and they hear some distant voices, saying, "Come and surf with us, Come and surf with us on the crystal shore." And the couple show up with surfboards in their arms and two surfboards for Surfersam and the other for Saltwatersally who are walking to the couple hand in hand and pick up the surfboards and surf the crystal shore.

The Newspaper and TV tell the sad story of the disappearance most loving surfing couple and how some swore that saw two coupled surfing at midnight, and it is said the surf the next day that the surf is great. The word gets out that people say they see the midnight surfers and tell their friends about it so when someone says they think they know where at a beach think they would show up on certain nights people pack up things to join in the others that make for parties. More and more people show up for the parties and even in different places around the world where there are waves. Some that took picture of them, Saltwatersally and Surfersam years ago, take their pictures of them enlarged and set them up at the party at the beaches where they first fell in love with each other and the one that has the picture that was look at the most was the one Salwatersally kiss after Surfersam had saved the boy that ran to his mother and ask Saltwatersally her to kiss her boyfriend for her Saltwatersally ran to kiss Surfersam. Most of the people started crying because they were so much in love, the people fell in love with the two. It was not long before people began asking for pictures to buy, mostly of the kiss but the ladies also wanted pictures of Surfersam, the men wanted pictures of Saltwatersally.

Today, many surfers go to the hotels where Saltwatersally and Surfersam had the last show before they disappeared. Many young lovers wanted pictures taken of them in the same spot that Saltwatersally kisse Surfersam. There were surfers that wanted weddings like Saltwatersally and Surfersam. Some bought statues of them kissing.

Did mid night surfing disappeared altogether? The answer is no. There are surfers with lights installed in their surfboards with lots of colors so may there be more shows at mid night and parties. It may be hotels putting on the show. Some still say they see Saltwatersally and Surfersam.

One thing surfers do, is to come up with new way to surf even in war or surfing on the street down, a snow covered maintain our out of an airplane, with a sale with down a sandy hill and much more.

As a long time, surfer, I got to ride thousands of waves and as a life guard had a wonderful summer of love that I will never forget. We were much younger that those in the story.

The answer is no we did not get married. I was only 17 and she was only 15 and 1/2.

I tried night surfing with big lights on the Oceanside pier but did not last very long.

Don't go away, there will be much more. I have to go and work on MY NEXT STORY, with a lady friend, but remember that this story belongs to Cramer Louis Jackson and will be made into the book by Toplink Publishers.

ON THE OTHER COUPLE THAT SURFS WITH THEM IS FROM THE MY BOOK "THE GIRLS OF MY IMAGINATION"

(THE CRYSTAL SHORE) page 47

I am dedicating this book to Gloria Nel Roberts that was the girl 15 1/2. I would like to thank all the wonderful surfers I got to surf with. And hope you all could fall in love like Saltwatersally and Surfersam.

Gloria 1956

lifegarding 1956 tent city beach

CPSIA information can be obtained
at www.ICGtesting.com
Printed in the USA
BVHW072337061218
534993BV00001B/23/P

9 781970 066364